A Note to Parents and Caregivers:

Read-it! Joke Books are for children who are moving ahead on the amazing road to reading. These fun books support the acquisition and extension of reading skills as well as a love of books.

Published by the same company that produces *Read-it!* Readers, these books introduce the question/answer pattern that helps children expand their thinking about language structure and book formats.

When sharing a book with your child, read in short stretches, pausing often to talk about the pictures and the meaning of the book. The question/answer format works well for this purpose and provides an opportunity to talk about the language and meaning of the jokes. Have your child turn the pages and point to the pictures and familiar words. Read the story in a natural voice; have fun creating the voices of characters or emphasizing some important words. And be sure to re-read favorite parts.

There is no right or wrong way to share books with children. Find time to read with your child and pass on the legacy of literacy.

Adria F. Klein, Ph.D.
Professor Emeritus
California State University
San Bernardino, California

Look for the other books in this series:

Chewy Chuckles: Deliciously Funny Jokes About Food (1-4048-0124-3)
Dino Rib Ticklers: Hugely Funny Jokes About Dinosaurs (1-4048-0122-7)
Galactic Giggles: Far-Out and Funny Jokes About Outer Space (1-4048-0126-X)
Monster Laughs: Frightfully Funny Jokes About Monsters (1-4048-0123-5)
School Buzz: Classy and Funny Jokes About School (1-4048-0121-9)

Editor: Nadia Higgins
Designer: John Moldstad
Page production: Picture Window Books
The illustrations in this book were prepared digitally.

Picture Window Books
5115 Excelsior Boulevard
Suite 232
Minneapolis, MN 55416
1-877-845-8392
www.picturewindowbooks.com

Printed in the United States of America.
1 2 3 4 5 6 08 07 06 05 04 03

Library of Congress Cataloging-in-Publication Data
Dahl, Michael.
Animal quack-ups : foolish and funny jokes about animals /
written by Michael Dahl ; illustrated by Jeff Yesh.
p. cm. — (Read-it! Joke Books)
Summary: An easy-to-read collection of jokes about ducks,
leopards, and other animals.
ISBN 1-4048-0125-1 (Library Binding)
1. Animals—Juvenile humor. 2. Wit and humor, Juvenile.
[1. Animals—Humor. 2. Riddles. 3. Jokes.] I. Yesh, Jeff, 1971- ill.
II. Title. III. Series.
PN6231.A5 D34 2003
818'.5402—dc21

2002156418

Animal Quack-Ups

Foolish and Funny Jokes About Animals

Michael Dahl • Illustrated by Jeff Yesh

Reading Advisers:
Adria F. Klein, Ph.D.
Professsor Emeritus, California State University
San Bernardino, California

Susan Kesselring, M.A., Literacy Educator
Rosemount-Apple Valley-Eagan (Minnesota) School District

What do you call two spiders that just got married?

Newlywebs.

What happened to the dog that ate a clock?

It got ticks.

Why did the little hummingbird have to stay after school?

He didn't do his humwork.

What happened when the cat swallowed a ball of yarn?

She had mittens.

What kind of dog enjoys taking a bath?

A shampoodle.

Why did the snake play with building blocks?

He was a boa constructor.

What happens to ducks when they fly upside down?

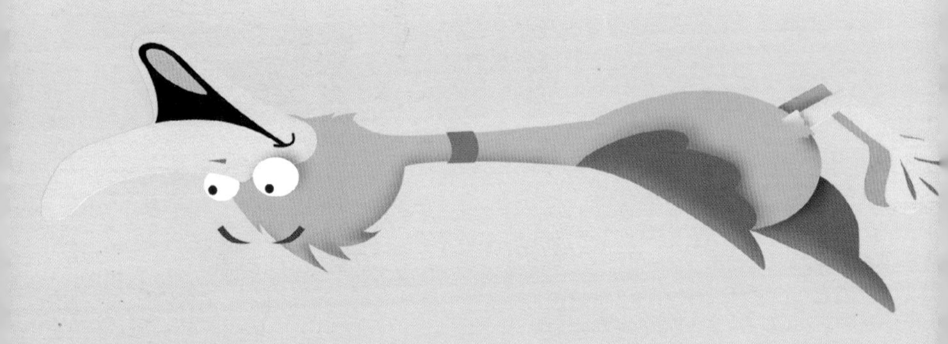

They quack up!

How can you tell that elephants like to swim?

They always have their trunks on.

What is a mouse's favorite game?

Hide and squeak.

What is the difference between an angry rabbit and a fake dollar bill?

One is a mad bunny,
and the other is bad money.

Where do cows go on vacation?

Moo-tels.

What did the leopard say after it ate a big meal?

"That hit the spots."

What did the duck say when it laid a square egg?

"Ouch!"

What's the worst thing about being an octopus?

 Washing your hands before dinner.

What do bees like to chew?

Bumble gum.

Why did the chicken cross the playground?

To get to the other slide.

Why was the centipede late for gym class?

She was tying her shoes.